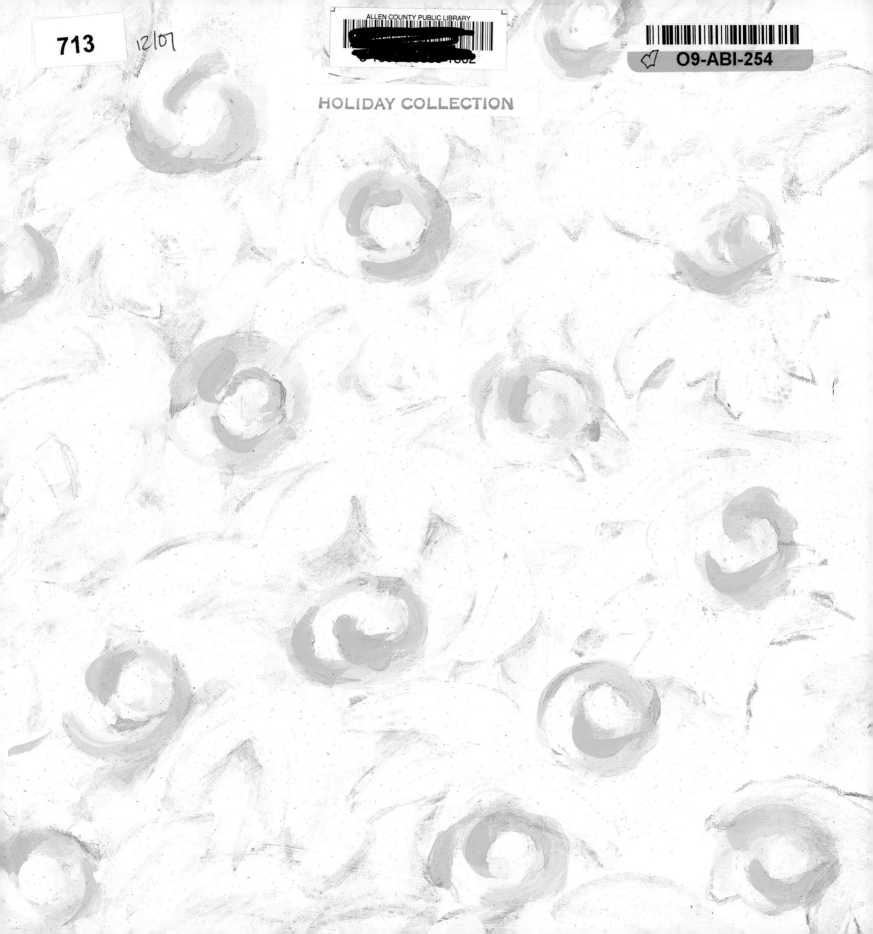

Christmas Is Coming

For Kathi and Annette
—A. B.

To my family, with gratitude for all Christmas memories
—T. B.

Carolrhoda Books, Inc.
A division of Lerner Publishing Group, Inc.
241 First Avenue North
Minneapolis, MN 55401 U.S.A.

Website address: www.lernerbooks.com

Library of Congress Cataloging-in-Publication Data

Bowen, Anne, 1952–
Christmas is coming / by Anne Bowen ; illustrated by Tomek Bogacki.
p. cm.
Summary: As a young girl eagerly awaits the arrival of Christmas, she describes to her new baby brother all of the wonderful ways in which her family prepares for this special holiday.
ISBN: 978–1–57505–934–1 (lib. bdg. : alk. paper)
[1. Christmas—Fiction. 2. Family life—Fiction. 3. Babies—Fiction.]
I. Bogacki, Tomek, ill. II. Title.
PZ7.B671945Ch 2007
[E] —dc22   2006035958

Manufactured in the United States of America
1 2 3 4 5 6 – JR – 12 11 10 09 08 07

Christmas Is Coming

BY ANNE BOWEN

ILLUSTRATIONS BY TOMEK BOGACKI

Carolrhoda Books, Inc.   Minneapolis · New York

You know Christmas is coming,
I tell my new baby brother,
when you wake up one morning
and know something is different.

You run to the window,
breathe a space in the frost,
and outside you see snow!
Falling,
swirling,
floating through the air.

You know Christmas is coming
when you see lights
like ribbons of stars shining in the dark—
glittering,
shimmering,
everywhere glimmering,
on trees and fences,
windows and doors,
all around the neighborhood!

When Mama brings out
the red berry wreath
and Daddy brings down boxes
from the closet, asking,
"Now, which one has the angel from Grandma?"

Then, I tell my new baby brother,
you know Christmas is coming!

Waiting for Christmas can be harder than
waiting for your birthday
or waiting for summer
or waiting for a visit
from Grandma and Grandpa.

But there are things you can do to help the waiting.

You can make cards.
Christmas cards for the neighbors,
for your friends,
even a card for the mailman.

Making presents can help the waiting too.
Presents for Mama and Daddy,
Grandma and Grandpa,
even Lucy, our cat.

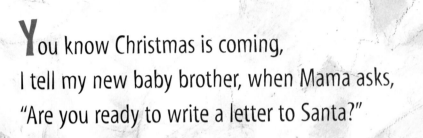

You know Christmas is coming,
I tell my new baby brother, when Mama asks,
"Are you ready to write a letter to Santa?"

Santa likes to know ahead of time
what you want for Christmas.
He likes to make sure
he has just the right present for you.
So every year, I spend a long time
thinking about my just-right present.

When I'm finished, I put Santa's letter in the mailbox.
Then I always ask Mama,
"How many more days until Christmas?"
And she always says, "Soon, Anna, very soon."

You know Christmas is getting closer,
I tell my new baby brother,
when Daddy says,
"Everyone into the car. It's time to get a tree!"

Along the way, you sing and sing:
"O Christmas tree! O Christmas tree!"
until Mama starts singing,
and then Daddy sings too,
and soon the car is cozy
and the windows foggy
from all that singing.

At the tree place,
you walk up and down
rows and rows of trees
looking for the perfect tree.

But . . . if you take too long,
I tell my new baby brother,
your body will get shivery,
your toes will get tingly,
and your ears will get all numbly.

So I am glad when I find our tree.
"Here it is!" I call out.
Mama says, "This is it."
Daddy says, "That's the one!"
And I say, "The best tree of all!"

At home, Daddy strings red and green
lights on the tree and Mama wraps chains
of silver beads all around it.

"Now your turn, Anna," she tells me.
I choose my favorite ornaments:
a cat that looks like Lucy,
three gold stars, and a bell
made out of glitter.

When we are finished,
Daddy holds me way up high,
so I can put Grandma's angel
at the very top.

And then our tree is ready for Christmas!

You know Christmas is *almost* here,
I tell my new baby brother,
when Grandma and Grandpa
come from their house
in the country
to our apartment
in the city.

We go caroling,
until our voices are tired
and our cheeks are rosy circles.
Then we hurry home,
ready for cookies and a toasty fire.

"Now how many days?" I ask Grandma.
Together we look at the calendar:
"1 . . . 2 . . . 3 . . . 4 . . . 5 days until Christmas!"

Making cookies to share with the neighbors
helps to make the days go faster.
Sugar cookies in all kinds of shapes:
stars and angels,
bells and wreaths,
even little reindeer.
And then—

FINALLY!

"It's Christmas Eve day, Anna," Mama says.
Only one more day of waiting!
One very,

      very,

         very

           long day.

And the night will feel even longer,
because you know Santa Claus is on his way.
You will lay in bed with your eyes wide open,
wiggling and squirming,
until slowly,

      slowly,

         you fall

           sound asleep. . . .

And when you wake up,
I tell my new baby brother,
it will be Christmas Day!

I always race down the stairs,
before anyone else,
and count all the presents under the tree.

Then I race back up the stairs,
to Mama and Daddy's room,
and shout, "Santa was here!"

That is sure to wake everyone up,
I tell my new baby brother.

There is a lot of hugging and laughing
as we all sit down around the tree,
ready to open presents because
EVERYONE likes presents on Christmas Day.

But this Christmas,
I tell my new baby brother,
there will be something different.
There will be something special
for all of us.

This Christmas
there will be YOU.
And that is
the best present of all!

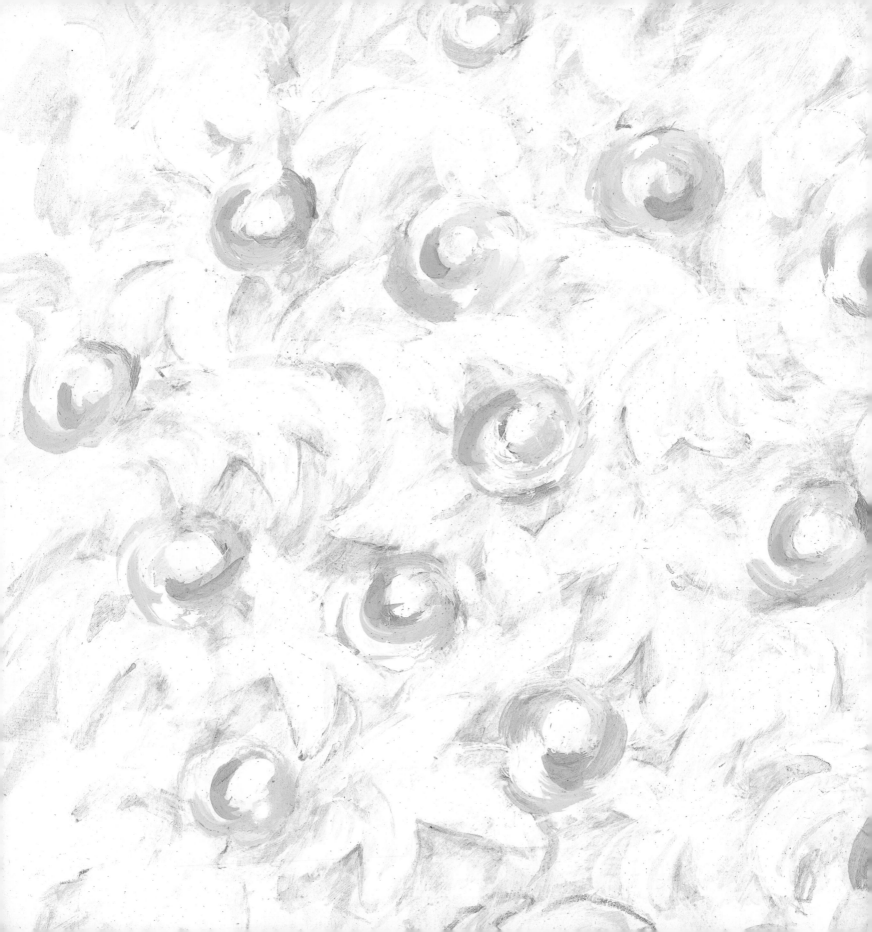